GIPSY MOTH

by Deannie Sullivan-Fraser

illustrations by HildaRose

This is a true story told to the author by her father, Johnny.

It is dedicated to the author's children
Sean, Michael and Maryanna,
grandchildren Kelly, Wylie and Maxwell
and all the children who dream of flying.

Johnny Sullivan was watching the Morrow brothers playing in the lane.

"You've been standing at that window for days, Johnny. Just go out and say hello," said his mother, handing him his best velvet jacket and nudging him out the door.

Slowly, Johnny opened the gate. His house in St. John's had always been filled with his cousins. This was the first time he had to ask someone else to play.

"Hi, I'm Johnny. I just moved here from St. John's."

"Lordie, lordie! Will ye look at the townie?" Kevin Morrow yelled.

All the Morrow boys drew around Johnny.

"Me mudder says you be a gentleman . . . are ye?" taunted Jimmy, tugging at Johnny's lace collar. All the Morrow boys laughed. They were dressed in hand-me-downs, patched sweaters and pants, and boots stuffed with newspaper so that they would fit.

"Can I play with ye?" Johnny asked,
taking a small step forward.

"No duckie! You'll get your *dress* dirty!"
jeered Georgie. They all laughed again.

For the first time in his life,
Johnny felt different.

"Stop tormentin' the youngster, you saucy
little crackies!" warned the postman,
walking up the lane. He handed Johnny
a parcel.

"Give this to your father, Master Johnny,
and mind now, don't go bending it . . .
there's something special inside."

Johnny hurried inside to the music room.
His father was playing his new song.
Johnny's heart soared with the melody.
When his father stopped to write down
the notes, Johnny handed him the parcel.

"This has come all the way from St. John's!"
said his father, handing Johnny the stamps
for his collection. His father reached in
and took out two folded white silk scarves.
Nestled between them were a letter and
a photograph.

"Look, lad!" he exclaimed, pointing to the
photograph. "This Gipsy Moth just made
the first air mail delivery from Canada!"

"What's a Gipsy Moth?" asked Johnny.

"A bi-plane, lad!" said his father pointing
to the sky. "Soon Gipsy Moths will be busy
flying mail and people across our great
country!"

"What are the scarves for?" asked Johnny. As
he twirled, they floated around him
like clouds.

"You'll find out soon enough, lad!"

His father pinned the photograph to the
wall. They stared in wonder as the Gipsy
Moth fluttered in the breeze from the
open window.

The next day Johnny came into the kitchen with a pot of glue and a spool of wire. His father carried an armful of wood and some fabric. They were going to make a Gipsy Moth. His father cut and glued the frame for the body, wings and tail. Johnny glued the fabric on the top.

"These posts are called struts – they keep the wings apart. Now let's put on the wires that will hold them together."

Johnny painted his Gipsy Moth bright yellow. He printed "Newfoundland Airways" in red along the side. When it was dry, he picked it up and ran through the kitchen. The propeller spun around and around. Forgetting his shyness, he burst out the back door and ran towards the Morrow boys.

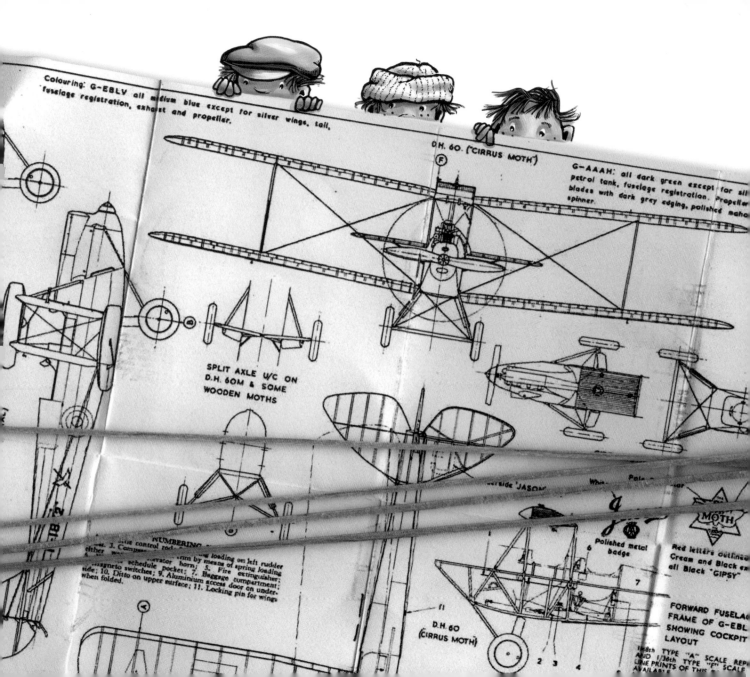

Colouring: G-EBLV all medium blue except for silver wings, tail,
fuselage registration, exhaust and propellar.

D.H. 60. ("CIRRUS MOTH")

G-AAAH: all dark green except for silver
petrol tank, fuselage registration. Propeller
blades with dark grey edging, polished maho...
spinner.

SPLIT AXLE U/C ON
D.H. 60M & SOME
WOODEN MOTHS

NUMBERING ...
...us control rod ... ...w loading on left rudder
...at. 3. Compas... ...mm by means of spring loading
either ... ...evator horn; 5. Fire extinguisher;
...schedule pocket; 7. Baggage compartment;
...magneto switches; 9. Aluminium access door on under-
side; 10. Ditto on upper surface; 11. Locking pin for wings
when folded.

...t side 'JASON'   Whi...   Pole...

Polished metal
badge

MOTH

Red letters outline...
Cream and Black ex...
all Black "GIPSY"

D.H. 60
(CIRRUS MOTH)

FORWARD FUSELA...
FRAME OF G-EBL...
SHOWING COCKPIT
LAYOUT

1/36th TYPE "A" SCALE RE...
AND 1/36th TYPE "B" SCA...
LINE PRINTS OF THIS ...
AVAILABLE ...

"It's a Gipsy Moth!" Johnny called out, excitedly.

"Lord, b'y!" sneered Kevin, "that's some hard lookin' butterfly!"

"Butterfly? Are you stunned? It's a moth! A Gipsy Moth!" yelled Johnny, mad as a hornet.

Johnny snapped around and stomped back into his house and up the stairs to the attic. He climbed up on top of his father's old trunk by the window. His new neighbourhood was spread out below him. Kevin was rolling a metal hoop. His brothers were chasing after it, trying to snatch it away with their sticks.

"I can run just as fast as ye!" he yelled, his voice bouncing back at him from the glass.

Johnny felt his heart grow small and cold. Disappointed, he lay down on the trunk and drifted off to sleep. He dreamed that he was landing his Gipsy Moth in St. John's. All his cousins were running out to meet him. *They* wanted to play pilot.

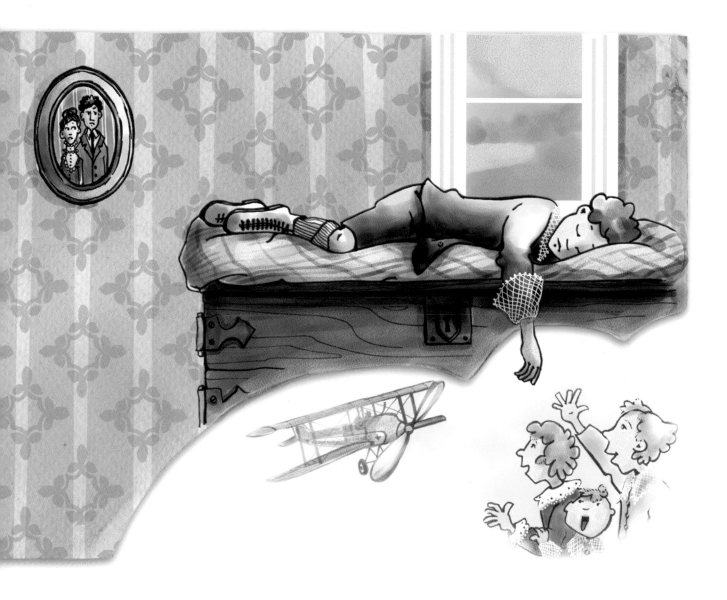

Suddenly, the window started rattling. Johnny's teeth started chattering, shaking him awake.

Everyone came rushing out of their houses. The women left their suppers boiling on their stoves. The men flung their axes to the ground. The Morrow boys tore up the lane as fast as they could. A plane was coming lower, closer! It was a moth, a Gipsy Moth, shining as yellow as the sun!

Johnny flew down the stairs then ran like the wind to Log Cabin Field. All the people of Grand Falls had gathered around the edge.

The Gipsy Moth came lower. It grew larger and larger. Finally the wheels touched the ground and a cloud of dust spit out behind as the plane's tail dragged along the bumpy field. The Gipsy Moth turned around and faced the crowd. The engine sputtered and the propeller stopped, as still as a fence post. A great cheer went up from the crowd.

Johnny strained to see as the pilot stood up in the cockpit. He looked like a giant insect with his bug-eyed goggles, leather helmet and white silk scarf.

"Greetings from the City of St. John's!" he shouted. The crowd cheered again. The Morrow boys tossed their caps into the air.

The pilot raised his hand for silence.

"Who among you is John M. Sullivan?"

Everyone gasped. The crowd parted, clearing a
path for Johnny, but he couldn't move. Jimmy
Morrow had to nudge him forward. When
Johnny stood below the Gipsy Moth,
he called up, "I am Johnny Sullivan, sir!"

"Well lad, no one goes flying dressed like that!"

Everybody laughed, but not for long.

"Try these on, young lad," said the pilot,
tossing Johnny a pair of bug-eyed goggles,
a leather helmet and
a white scarf of his own.
Now, up you come!"

Johnny's neighbours hoisted him up to the cockpit. Through a tube in the helmet Johnny heard the pilot say, "Welcome aboard Newfoundland Airways, Master Johnny. I'm your Uncle Arthur. You're about to learn what the birds already know!"

Uncle Arthur asked Mr. Morrow to grab the propeller and give it a spin.

"Contact!" Uncle Arthur yelled. The crowd drew back as the mighty engine roared to life.

The Gipsy Moth moved slowly at first. Johnny's teeth rattled and clacked as they crossed the bumpy field. Faster and faster they went. The wind set their silk scarves a'snapping. Everything streaked by in a blur. Johnny's tummy sank to his knees as the Gipsy Moth broke free of the ground and soared up into the cool, blue sky.

Johnny saw his neighbourhood far below. His house was no bigger than a junk of wood. His parents, no bigger than toy soldiers, were waving with the scarves that had come in the mail. Uncle Arthur waggled the Gipsy Moth's wings in reply.

Grand Falls was spread out below them like a blanket. The Exploits River was the size of a snake, shining as silver as the fish scales in Johnny's pocket. The Gipsy Moth's shadow slithered along its back.

The gasoline and the oil smelled sweeter than any perfume. The engine beat a rhythm that made the instruments dance. The wind rushing past the wires filled the air with the song of a thousand violins.

"I'm alive!" yelled Johnny, spreading his arms like a bird. He was filled with the song of the Gipsy Moth.

Uncle Arthur raised one wing higher than the other. The Gipsy Moth drew a large circle in the sky. Johnny's new town wheeled below him until Uncle Arthur lined the Gipsy Moth up with Log Cabin Field.

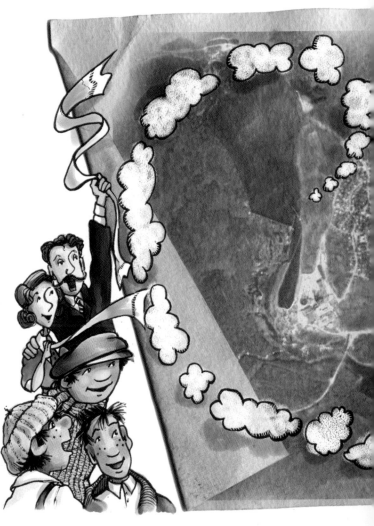

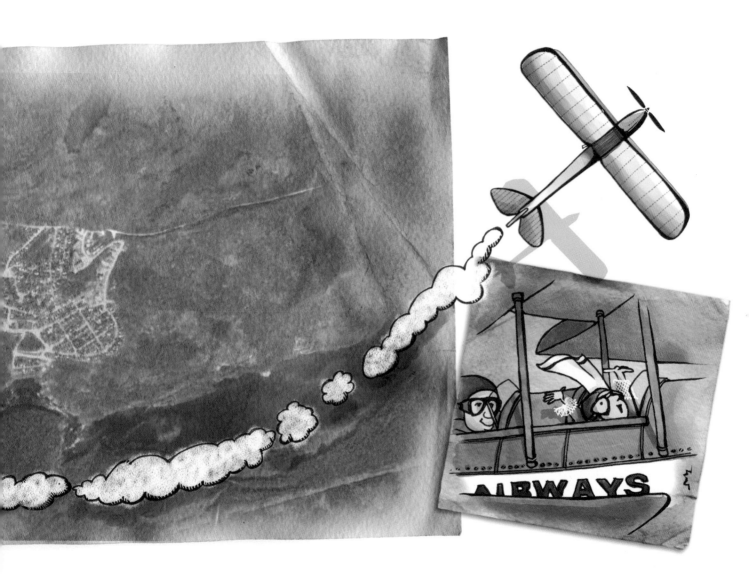

The Gipsy Moth went lower and lower. The trees became larger and larger. The grass came up to meet them and the wheels smacked onto the ground. Johnny's teeth rattled and clacked as they taxied up the field.

The engine sputtered to a stop. The crowd burst into cheers. The Morrow boys tossed their caps wildly into the air.

Uncle Arthur shook Johnny's hand, and then lowered him down to his neighbours.

"Thank you, sir!" Johnny called up, filled with happiness. "Will you be coming up to the house?"

"I've got mail to deliver, nephew! Won't the people of St. Anthony be surprised at how fast it arrives?"

Johnny took off his helmet, goggles and his scarf and held them up to his uncle.

"Keep them, lad. You never know when you'll need them again."

Once again, Uncle Arthur asked Mr. Morrow to give the propeller a spin.

"Contact!" yelled Uncle Arthur as the Gipsy Moth roared to life.

The plane bobbled down the field, then rose effortlessly into the air. The crowd watched, spellbound, until the Gipsy Moth became a small, yellow insect humming in the clear blue sky.

Johnny turned to go. The Morrow boys, who had wormed their way to the front of the crowd, shyly took a step towards him. They wanted to say something but their tongues were glued to the roofs of their mouths. Johnny, whose heart had grown big enough to hold a Gipsy Moth, made the first move.

"Kevin, do you want to try the goggles?"

And to Georgie, "Do you to want to try on the helmet?"

Then to Jimmy, "Would you like to wear the scarf?"

Jimmy smiled and tipped his cap. "Now, Master Johnny, I knows you be a gentleman!"

The next day, the Morrow boys carried yaffles of wood to the lane. Johnny brought fabric and glue pots and paint. Together, they built a platform in the big tree above their lane.

"Contact!" they yelled. Then Johnny and the Morrow boys, their Gipsy Moths filled with passengers and mail, flew off into the great Newfoundland sky.

Newfoundland Words

Crackie   A small, yappy little dog that bites at your ankles.

Fish scales   The name given to Newfoundland's small, silver 5 cent coin.

Stunned   Foolish or stupid.

Townie   What someone from the outports calls someone from the city of St. John's.

Yaffles   Armloads.

Ye   An older way of saying you.

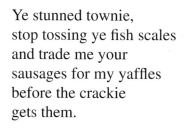

Ye stunned townie, stop tossing ye fish scales and trade me your sausages for my yaffles before the crackie gets them.

Canada Council
for the Arts

Conseil des Arts
du Canada

Newfoundland
Labrador

We gratefully acknowledge the financial support of
The Canada Council for the Arts, the Government
of Canada through the Book Publishing Industry
Development Program (BPIDP), and the Government of
Newfoundland and Labrador through the Department
of Tourism, Culture and Recreation for our publishing
program.

Illustrations ©2009, Kathy (HildaRose) Kaulbach
Design and layout by Kathy Kaulbach

Published by

Tuckamore Books
a Creative Publishers imprint

A Transcontinental Inc. associated company
P.O. Box 8660, Station A
St. John's, Newfoundland A1B 3T7

Printed in Canada by: Transcontinental Inc.

**Library and Archives Canada Cataloguing
in Publication**

Sullivan-Fraser, Deannie
Johnny and the Gypsy Moth / Deannie Sullivan-Fraser
illustrated by Hilda Rose.

ISBN 978-1-897174-40-1

I. Rose, Hilda, 1955- II. Title.
PS8637.U559J65 2009   jC813'.6   C2009-900602-2